STERLING and the distinctive Sterling logo are
registered trademarks of Sterling Publishing Co., Inc.

Library of Congress Cataloging-in-Publication Data

Gow, Nancy.
Ten big toes and a prince's nose / Nancy Gow ; illustrated by Stephen Costanza.
p. cm.
Summary: A lovely princess with enormous feet and a charming prince with a huge nose meet on
a ski lift and, while their flaws are hidden, fall in love.
ISBN 978-1-4027-6396-0 (alk. paper)
[1. Stories in rhyme. 2. Individuality–Fiction. 3. Self-confidence–Fiction. 4. Princesses–Fiction. 5.
Princes–Fiction.] I. Costanza, Stephen, ill. II. Title.
PZ8.3.G7197Ten 2010
[E]–dc22
                                                        2008031835

Lot#:
2   4   6   8   10   9   7   5   3   1
4/10

Published by Sterling Publishing Co., Inc.
387 Park Avenue South, New York, NY 10016
Text © 2010 by Nancy Gow
Illustrations © 2010 by Stephen Costanza
Distributed in Canada by Sterling Publishing
c/o Canadian Manda Group, 165 Dufferin Street
Toronto, Ontario, Canada M6K 3H6
Distributed in the United Kingdom by GMC Distribution Services
Castle Place, 166 High Street, Lewes, East Sussex, England BN7 1XU
Distributed in Australia by Capricorn Link (Australia) Pty. Ltd.
P.O. Box 704, Windsor, NSW 2756, Australia

Printed in China
All rights reserved

Sterling ISBN 978-1-4027-6396-0

For information about custom editions, special sales, premium and
corporate purchases, please contact Sterling Special Sales
Department at 800-805-5489 or specialsales@sterlingpublishing.com.

Jacket and interior design by Chrissy Kwasnik
Illustrations were created with pastels on masonite board

Ten Big Toes and a Prince's Nose

By Nancy Gow   Illustrated by Stephen Costanza

STERLING

New York / London

To Bernie, with gratitude;
to Lucille, the original big-footed princess;
and to Anne, Willie, and Wanda, with love. —N.G.

To Mom & Dad, Happy Anniversary, with love. —S.C.

There once was a princess so lovely and fair
with ruby red lips and a mane of brown hair.
Her voice was like honey, her smile soft and sweet...

. . . but the beautiful princess had **gigantic** feet.

Her feet were so large that each prince who dropped by
ran straight for the door. They would not even try
to find out how charming a princess can be—
for her gigantic feet were the first thing they'd see.

But still there was hope, for the princess's mom was a clever old gal who would say to her, "Hon, my mother would sing me a rhyme every night just before she would kiss me and turn out the light:

I am what I am and that's all right with me.
I don't have to be different, I just have to be.
I don't want to be somebody else. No sir-ree!
I am what I am and that's all right with me."

Now far, far away in our fanciful yarn,
there lived a young prince with a nose like a barn.
The prince loved to laugh.
He was bright like the sun.
He was warm, he was kind,
he was charming and fun.

But maidens rebuffed him.
They'd look at his beak
and say, "Oops, gotta run!"
before he would speak.

They never found out
how much fun he could be
for a gigantic nose was
the first thing they'd see.

But still there was hope, for the prince had a dad who was clever and wise. He would say to him, "Lad, my father would sing me a rhyme every night just before he would kiss me and turn out the light:

I am what I am and that's all right with me.
I don't have to be different, I just have to be.
I don't want to be somebody else. No sir-ree!
I am what I am and that's all right with me."

One day, while the princess was skiing in France,
His Wonderful Highness just happened to glance
at the beautiful girl who glided with ease
down the slopes of the Alps. (She was not wearing skis.)

The princess meanwhile saw the prince all aglow.
(His scarf was so big that his nose didn't show.)
They met on a ski lift that whizzed high above,
and then bells started ringing!
And choirs were singing!

The prince and the princess fell deeply in love.

The prince was enthralled by the princess's smile,
her beautiful voice and her princess-y style.
The princess laughed hard at His Highness's wit.
She enjoyed a good joke. The young prince was a hit!

But when the night deepened, the ski hill had closed.
The prince knew he'd have to reveal his big nose.

It was time for the princess, lovely and fair,
to reveal that she didn't have skis way down there.

The prince shook with fear.

There was sweat on his brow.

To win the fair princess he'd have to act now.

He thought of the words that his father had said
and he slowly unraveled the scarf from his head . . .

And oh, he was happy! So happy was he
when he looked at the princess and all he could see
were two shining eyes and a smile that was sweet
and a pair of humongous un-princess-like feet!

He stared at her toes. She stared at his nose.
They laughed and they giggled, and then he proposed.

They rode to his castle for crumpets and tea,
and they both were as happy as happy could be.

So if, one fine day, you should happen to meet
a guy with a schnoz and a gal with big feet,
don't jump to conclusions, try not to be mean . . .

. . . for you might have bumped into
a **king** and a **queen!**

The End